1483/
1.8?

398.2/ Cheng, Hou-tien
CHE
     Six Chinese brothers

S0-AAE-044

DATE DUE

MAR 1 7 1989	MAR 2 4 1992
JAN 2 6 1990	
APR 3 Y MAR 5 1991	
	2/5 (6+L)
FEB 1 9 2001	

© THE BAKER & TAYLOR CO.

SIX CHINESE BROTHERS
An Ancient Tale

by Cheng Hou-tien

illustrated with scissor cuts by the author

Holt, Rinehart and Winston / New York

Copyright © 1979 by Cheng Hou-tien / All rights reserved,
including the right to reproduce this book or portions
thereof in any form. / Published simultaneously in Canada
by Holt, Rinehart and Winston of Canada, Limited.
Printed in the United States of America
10 9 8 7 6 5 4 3 2 1   14831

Library of Congress Cataloging in Publication Data

Cheng, Hou-tien   Six Chinese brothers: An Ancient Tale
SUMMARY: Six look-alike Chinese brothers, each with a
special talent, manage to outwit the king's executioner.
[1. Folklore—China] I. Title   PZ8.1.C397Si
398.2'1'0951 [E]   79-1218   ISBN 0-03-048311-5

SIX CHINESE BROTHERS

Long ago, in ancient China, lived an old farmer with his six sons. The first son was clever.

The second son could stretch his arms to either end of the world.

The third son had a head so hard, steel bounced off it.

The fourth son had skin like iron.

The fifth son could withstand the greatest heat.

And the sixth son, why he was able to stretch his legs for inches and feet and yards—and for miles and miles.

One day the old farmer fell ill. None of the doctors could cure him. "There is only one way to save your father," said one. "You must get the pearl from the king's palace, boil it in water, and give your father the water to drink."

First Son said, "Second Son, stretch out your arms and get the pearl."

Second Son reached out across the plains....

....into the city, where the palace was....

....and into the king's window and drew out the pearl.

The brothers boiled the pearl....

....and gave their father the water to drink, and the old man got better.

When the king discovered that his precious pearl was missing, he was furious.

He sent his soldiers to find it.

They went from door to door.
When First Son opened the
door and the soldiers saw
the pearl, they seized it.

And they arrested First Son and brought him before the king.
"Off with his head!" cried the king.
First Son could not stand the thought of dying without seeing
his father one more time.
"Please let me see my father before I die," he begged. The
king allowed him to go.

When the old farmer learned that his son was to be beheaded, he was very sad. "But wait," said Third Son. "Let me go and take my brother's place."

The next day, it was Third Son who put his head on the
block. The executioner lowered the ax, but the head re-
mained. The people laughed and jeered.

The king was angry. He ordered his soldiers to run him through with a knife. Third Son was frightened. "Please let me see my father before I die," he said.

The king allowed him to go. When the brothers heard the news, it was suggested that Fourth Son go back instead. This, Fourth Son did.

And the next day, when the soldiers brought the knife down on him, the blade snapped in two, like a bamboo stick.

"Throw him into boiling water," cried the king.
"That will finish him off."
"Please let me go home
and see my father
before I die,"
Fourth Son pleaded.

The next day, when Fifth Son was thrown into boiling water, to the great surprise of all around, he merely called for more heat and began to sing.

The king sputtered and railed. "Throw him into the sea! No one escapes from its depth," he cried.

"I accept my fate," said Fifth Son. "But before I die, please let me go home and see my father."

Fifth Son hurried home and told what had happened.
"Never mind," said First Son. "Sixth Son will take your place.
He can never drown."

Sixth Son returned to the palace in his brother's place. He was taken out to sea and dropped overboard. The soldiers watched him disappear. They saw bubbles form on the surface of the water and were sure he had drowned.

But Sixth Son was far from gone. He stretched and stretched his legs until he was standing on the ocean floor. There, he found many precious jewels. When he rose to the surface, the surprised soldiers brought him to the king.

Sixth Son presented the king with the jewels he had found.
The jewels pleased the king and he decided to spare the
boy's life.

"How is it that you have escaped sure death again and
again?" asked the king. When the king heard the story, he
sent for the other five brothers and said, "You boys are a fine
example of devotion to family. China is proud of you."

And he held a banquet for the old farmer and his six sons at the palace, which hundreds of people attended.